More Than Two Hands Full

by Jerry and Kitty Thomas
ILLUSTRATED BY KIM JUSTINEN

Edited by B. Russell Holt
Designed by Kim Justinen
Illustrated by Kim Justinen
Typeset in Century 20/26

Printed in the United States of America

www.adventistbookcenter.com

ISBN: 0-8163-1953-7

02 03 04 05 06 • 5 4 3 2 1

Max sat on the floor of his room. His face
was twisted into a pout. "They're my aminals,"
he said. He reached over and picked up a blue

bear, a red monkey, and a goat.

"Come on, Bluey. Come on, Spike and Angelo. You're going back under my bed."

Mom backed out of his closet with another box. "Animals, Max," she reminded him. "Look, here are more that you don't play with anymore. How many animals do you need to have?"

Max reached into the box with both hands. "I don't have enough efalunts or rhineroceroses or zedras," he said.

Mom shook her head. "You mean you don't have enough elephants or rhinoceroses or zebras," she said.

"That's what I said," Max agreed. Max was used to getting things mixed up.

Sometimes words turned themselves around when he said them. Sometimes he ended up with different colored socks on his feet.

Sometimes his friends called him "Mixed-up Max."

"Which ones do you want to share with the Children's Home?" Mom asked.

Max tried to scoop up all the animals at once, but some fell to the floor. "If I share, there won't be enough for me," he said quietly.

Mom knelt down on the floor next to him. "Max, we share our things with others every year at Thanksgiving time.

"Remember the story of the little boy who shared his lunch with Jesus? And remember how the American Indians and the Pilgrims

shared their food? Sharing is what
Thanksgiving is about. Can't we share some
of these animals with other children?"

Max thought about other children not hav-
ing any toys to play with. It made him feel
sad. But giving away his animals made him
feel sad too. "Do I have to give all my animals
away?" he asked quietly.

Mom hugged him. "Let's make a deal,
Max. We'll take the whole box to Mrs. Bickett
at the Children's Home, but you'll decide how

many to give away. We'll bring the rest back with us."

As they drove up to the Children's Home, Max held on to his big box with both hands. Kids were playing kickball in the big front yard. "Why don't you leave your box in the car for now?" Mom said. "Go see what the kids are doing."

Max waved to Mrs. Bickett, then sat on the porch and watched the game. A wild kick sent the ball bouncing right to him. The girl who chased it smiled at him. "Hi! What's your name?" she asked.

Max bounced the ball to her. "I'm Max," he said.

"I'm Sophie," she told him. "You wanna play?"

Later, when they came inside, Max ran to his mother. "Mom, Mom! You should have seen how far I kicked that ball! And when I got mixed up and ran to the wrong base, they said it was OK! They didn't care which base I ran to! So I got a home run!"

Mom smiled. "It sounds like you made some friends, Max."

Max ran back to find Sophie standing by a big fish tank. "What do we play now?" he asked.

Sophie frowned. "There's not much to do when we come inside," she said. "Mostly we just pretend. I like to play zookeeper over here by the fish tank. I pretend this fish is my shark, and this big one is my whale. The other animals stay over in the corner in their cages. Wanna play zookeeper?"

Max's eyes started to twinkle. Then he turned and ran to the kitchen. "Mom! Mom, come on! We have to get my box from the car."

Out at the car, Mom helped Max lift the box. "Are you sure this is what you want to do?" she asked.

"I'm sure," Max said with a big smile.

"Sophie, look what I brought," he said. Sophie watched while he opened the box and pulled out an elephant and a rhinoceros. "Efalunts and rhineroceroses," he said. "For your zoo."

Now Sophie had a big smile. She reached down into the box and brought out two handfuls of animals. "I'll have the best pretend zoo ever!" she said.

Soon other kids were crowding around. Mom and Mrs. Bickett watched from the doorway. "I want an animal, too," a girl said. But when she reached for one, Sophie snatched it away.

"No! They're my animals!" she cried.

Max shook his head. "I brought the animals for everyone to play with," he said.

Mrs. Bickett put her hand on Sophie's shoulder. "Thank you, Max, for bringing your animals. Sophie, I'm sure you want to share with everyone."

Sophie held both handfuls of animals as tight as she could. "But if I share, there won't be enough for me," she said.

Max looked at her. "Don't you know the story of the first Thanksgiving, when the boy shared his food with Jesus?"

Sophie shook her head. "No," she said. So Max told her the story.

"When the Pilgrims sailed across the sea on their big ship, they found Jesus talking to His friends.

They all sat down to listen to His stories.

"After a while, they got very hungry. But no one had any food.

"Jesus said, 'We need to feed these people. Invite them all to sit down at our table.' So His friends found chairs for everyone, but they still didn't have any food.

"They said, 'Jesus, only one boy brought food. He has two loaves of bread and three fish.'

Sophie stopped the story. "Did he have fish like mine?" she asked.

"Yes," Max said.

"What was he going to do with all that bread?" she asked. "Make a lot of sandwiches?"

"I guess," Max said. "But then he saw that no one else had any food. He said, 'I'm afraid if I share, there won't be enough for me. But I guess I could share, because it's Thanksgiving.' "

Max looked up and smiled at his mom. She smiled back.

"So the boy took his bread and his fish to Jesus. Jesus said 'Thank you.' Then He prayed and said 'Thank You' to God. Then Jesus handed the fish and the bread to His

friends and said, 'Take some, then share the bread with
the next person.'

"Jesus' friends said, 'If we share, there won't be

enough for us.' But Jesus said, 'When we share, there's always enough for everyone.'

"So each of Jesus' friends took a piece of bread and

passed it on to the next person. Everyone got a piece, but the bag was never empty!

"When they collected the leftover bread and brought it

back to the boy, he had more bread than he could hold in both hands! So he let everyone take some home."

Sophie stopped the story again. "What happened to his fish?" she asked.

Max smiled. "Hmmm . . . I guess he gave everyone a bag of fish to take home too. And that's the story of the first Thanksgiving."

Max looked up to see his mom and Mrs. Bickett smiling. Mom said, "Your story was a little mixed up, Max, but you were exactly right. Look what Jesus gave you when you decided to share your toys."

Max looked at his mom for a second. Then he smiled even bigger than before. He picked up two hands full of animals and started handing them out. "Happy Thanksgiving!" he said to all his new friends.

Jesus said:

"When you share, you get more back than you give away. You'll get more than you can hold in both hands! The way you share with others is the way God shares with you."

Did you figure out what Jesus gave Max when he shared? More friends than he could put both his arms around! The story of the miracle of the bread and fishes is found in Luke 9:10-17. Jesus' promise is from Luke 6:38.